One day he saw the bear sitting on the mantelpiece and it sparked an idea: *"When I wrote those few words, I had no idea quite what a change they would eventually make to my life. It was really a case of putting something down on paper in order to get my brain working that morning."* Michael soon found that he had a book on his hands, and in 1958 *A Bear Called Paddington* was published with many, many more stories to follow.

Sixty years later, the Paddington books have sold over thirty-five million copies worldwide and been translated into over forty different languages. Paddington continues to touch the hearts of readers worldwide with his earnest good intentions and humorous misadventures, and has even starred in two blockbuster movies.

Michael Bond was awarded an OBE in July 1997 and then a CBE in June 2015. He died in June 2017, leaving behind one of the great literary legacies of our time.

by the same author

A Bear Called Paddington

More About Paddington

Paddington Helps Out

Paddington Abroad

Paddington at Large

Paddington Marches On

Paddington at Work

Paddington Goes to Town

Paddington Takes the Air

Paddington on Top

Paddington Takes the Test

Paddington Here and Now

Paddington Races Ahead

Love from Paddington

Paddington's Finest Hour

Paddington
Turns Detective
and Other Funny Stories

This book belongs to:

I celebrated *World Book Day* with this brilliant gift from my local Bookseller and HarperCollins Children's Books.

Michael Bond was born in Newbury, Berkshire, in January 1926. He served in both the Royal Air Force and the Middlesex Regiment of the British Army during the Second World War. He first began writing in 1945 when he was in the Army, selling his first short story to a magazine called *London Opinion* for seven guineas.

On Christmas Eve, 1956, while working as a BBC cameraman, Michael bought a small toy bear which had been left alone on a shelf in a London department store. Feeling sorry for it, he took it home and gave it to his wife. They lived near Paddington station and Michael had often thought that Paddington would make a good name for a character.

CELEBRATE STORIES. LOVE READING.

This book has been specially compiled and published to celebrate **World Book Day**. We are a charity which offers every child and young person the opportunity to read and love books by giving you the chance to have a book of your own. For more information, and oodles of fun activities and recommendations to continue your reading journey, visit **worldbookday.com**

World Book Day in the UK and Ireland is made possible by generous sponsorship from National Book Tokens, participating publishers, booksellers, authors and illustrators. The £1* book tokens are a gift from your local Bookseller.

World Book Day works in partnership with a number of charities, all of whom are striving to encourage a love of reading for pleasure.

The National Literacy Trust is an independent charity that encourages children to enjoy reading. Just ten minutes of reading every day can make a big difference to how well you do at school and how successful you could be in life. **literacytrust.org.uk**

The Reading Agency inspires people of all ages and backgrounds to read for pleasure and empowerment. They run the Summer Reading Challenge in partnership with libraries, as well as supporting reading groups in schools and libraries all year round. Find out more and join your local library at **summerreadingchallenge.org.uk**

World Book Day also facilitates fundraising for:

Book Aid International, an international book donation and library development charity. Every year, they provide one million books to libraries and schools in communities where children would otherwise have little or no opportunity to read. **bookaid.org.uk**

Read for Good, which motivates children in schools to read for fun through its sponsored read, run by thousands of schools on World Book Day and throughout the year. The money raised provides new books and resident storytellers in all of the UK's children's hospitals. **readforgood.org**

*€1.50 in Ireland

This edition first published in paperback in Great Britain
by HarperCollins Children's Books in 2018

Paddington Turns Detective from *More About Paddington* first published
in Great Britain by HarperCollins*Publishers* Ltd in 1959
Revised editions published by Collins in 1997 and HarperCollins Children's Books
in 2003, 2014 and 2017

A Spot of Fishing from *Paddington Abroad* first published in Great Britain
by HarperCollins*Publishers* Ltd in 1961
Revised editions published by Collins in 1997 and HarperCollins Children's Books
in 2003, 2014 and 2017

An Unexpected Party from *Paddington Marches On* first published in Great Britain
by HarperCollins*Publishers* Ltd in 1964
Revised editions published by HarperCollins Children's Books in 1998, 2014 and 2017

1 3 5 7 9 10 8 6 4 2

Collins is an imprint of HarperCollins Children's Books Ltd.
HarperCollins Children's Books is a division of HarperCollins*Publishers* Ltd,
1 London Bridge Street, London SE1 9GF.

Visit our website at:
www.harpercollins.co.uk

Cover illustrations adapted and coloured by Mark Burgess
from the originals by Peggy Fortnum

ISBN: 978-0-00-827980-6

Originated by Dot Gradations Ltd, UK
Printed in Great Britain by
CPI Group (UK) Ltd, Croydon CR0 4YY

MIX
Paper from
responsible sources
FSC™ C007454

This book is produced from independently certified FSC™ paper
to ensure responsible forest management.

For more information visit: www.harpercollins.co.uk/green

Paddington
Turns Detective
and Other Funny Stories

Michael Bond

Illustrated by Peggy Fortnum

HarperCollins *Children's Books*

Contents

Paddington
Turns Detective
from *More About Paddington*

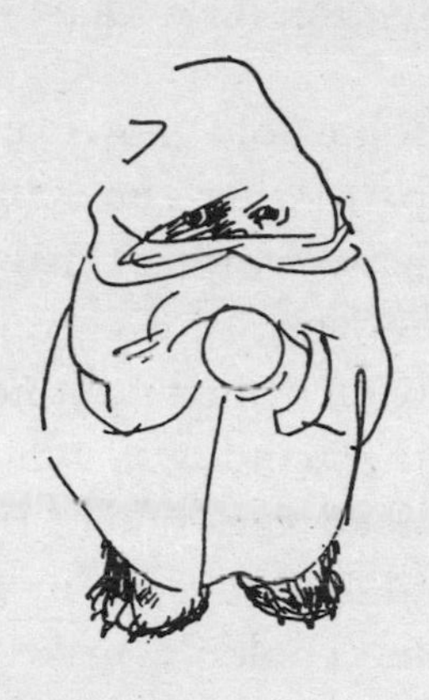

Paddington Turns Detective

The old box-room was finished at last and everyone, including Paddington, agreed that he was a very lucky bear to move into such a nice room. Not only was the paintwork a gleaming white, so that he could almost see his face in it, but the walls were gaily papered and he even had new furniture of his own as well.

"In for a penny, in for a pound!" Mr Brown had said. And he had bought Paddington a brand-new bed with special short legs, a spring mattress, and a cupboard for his odds and ends.

There were several other pieces of furniture and Mrs Brown had been extravagant and bought a thick pile carpet for the floor. Paddington was very proud of his carpet and he'd carefully spread

some old newspapers over the parts where he walked so that his paws wouldn't make it dirty.

Mrs Bird's contribution had been some bright new curtains for the windows, which Paddington liked very much. In fact, the first night he spent in his new room he couldn't make up his mind whether to have them drawn together so that he could admire them, or left apart so that he could see the view. He got out of bed several times and eventually decided to have one drawn and the other left back so that he could have the best of both worlds.

Then something strange caught his eye. Paddington made a point of keeping a torch by the side of his bed in case there was an emergency during the night, and it was while he was flashing it on and off to admire the drawn curtain that he noticed it. Each time he flashed the torch there was an answering flicker of light from somewhere outside. He sat up in bed, rubbing his eyes, and stared in the direction of the window.

He decided to try a more complicated signal.

Two short flashes followed by several long ones. When he did so he nearly fell out of bed with surprise, for each time he sent a signal it was repeated in exactly the same way through the glass.

Paddington jumped out of bed and rushed to the window. He stayed there for a long while peering out at the garden, but he couldn't see anything at all. Having made sure the window was tightly shut, he drew both curtains and hurried back to bed, pulling the clothes over his head a little farther than usual. It was all very mysterious and Paddington didn't believe in taking any chances.

It was Mr Brown, at breakfast next morning, who gave him his first clue.

"Someone's stolen my prize marrow!" he announced crossly. "They must have got in during the night."

For some weeks past Mr Brown had been carefully nursing a huge marrow which he intended to enter for a vegetable show. He watered it morning and evening and measured it every night before going to bed.

Mrs Brown exchanged a glance with Mrs Bird. "Never mind, Henry, dear," she said. "You've got several others almost as good."

"I *do* mind," grumbled Mr Brown. "And the others will never be as good – not in time for the show."

"Perhaps it was one of the other competitors, Dad," said Jonathan. "Perhaps they didn't want you to win. It was a jolly good marrow."

"That's quite possible," said Mr Brown, looking more pleased at the thought. "I've a good mind to offer a small reward."

Mrs Bird hastily poured out some more tea. Both she and Mrs Brown appeared anxious to change the subject. But Paddington pricked up his ears at the mention of a reward. As soon as he had finished his toast and marmalade he asked to be excused and disappeared upstairs

without even having a third cup of tea.

It was while she was helping Mrs Bird with the washing-up that Mrs Brown first noticed something odd going on in the garden.

"Look!" she said, nearly dropping one of the breakfast plates in her astonishment. "Behind the cabbage patch. Whatever is it?"

Mrs Bird followed her gaze out of the window to where something brown and shapeless kept bobbing up and down. Her face cleared. "It's Paddington," she said. "I'd recognise his hat anywhere."

"Paddington?" echoed Mrs Brown. "But what on earth is he doing crawling about in the cabbage patch on his paws and knees?"

"He looks as if he's lost something," said Mrs Bird. "That's Mr Brown's magnifying glass he's got."

Mrs Brown sighed. "Oh well, we shall know what it is soon enough, I expect."

Unaware of the interest he was causing, Paddington sat down behind a raspberry cane and undid a small notebook which he opened at a page marked LIST OF CLEWS.

Recently Paddingon had been reading a mystery story which Mr Gruber had lent him and he had begun to fancy himself as a detective. The mysterious flashes of the night before and the loss of Mr Brown's marrow convinced him his opportunity had come at last.

So far it had all been rather disappointing. He had found several footprints, but he'd traced them all back to the house. In the big gap left by Mr Brown's prize marrow there were two dead beetles and an empty seed packet, but that was all.

All the same, Paddington wrote the details carefully in his notebook and drew a map of the garden – putting a large X to mark the spot where the marrow had once been. Then he went back upstairs to his room in order to think things out. When he got there he made another addition to his map – a drawing of the new house

which was being built beyond the edge of the garden. Paddington decided that was where the mysterious flashes must have come from the night before. He stared at it through his opera glasses for some time but the only people he could see were the builders.

Shortly afterwards, anyone watching the Browns' house would have seen the small figure of a bear emerge from the front door and make its way towards the market. Fortunately for Paddington's plans no one saw him leave, nor did anyone see him when he returned some while later carrying a large parcel in his arms. There was an excited gleam in his eyes as he crept back up the stairs and entered his bedroom, carefully locking the door behind him. Paddington liked parcels and this one was particularly interesting.

It took him a long time to undo the knots on the string, because his paws were trembling with excitement, but when he did pull the paper apart it revealed a long cardboard box, very brightly coloured, with the words MASTER DETECTIVE'S DISGUISE OUTFIT on the front.

Paddington had been having a battle with himself ever since he'd first seen it several days before in a shop window. Although seven pounds seemed an awful lot of money to pay for anything – especially when you only get one pound a week pocket money – Paddington felt very pleased with himself as he emptied the contents on to the floor. There was a long black beard, some dark glasses, a police whistle, several bottles of chemicals marked 'Handle with Care' – which Paddington hurriedly put back in the box – a finger-print pad, a small bottle of invisible ink, and a book of instructions.

It seemed a very good disguise outfit. Paddington tried writing his name on the lid of the box with the invisible ink and he couldn't see it at all. Then he tested the finger-print pad with his paw and blew several blasts on the police whistle under the bedclothes. He rather wished he'd thought of doing it the other way round as a lot of the ink came off on the sheets, which was going to be difficult to explain.

But he liked the beard best of all. It had two pieces of wire for fitting over the ears, and when he turned and suddenly caught sight of himself in the mirror it quite made him jump. With his hat on, and an old raincoat of Jonathan's which Mrs Brown had put out for the jumble sale, he could hardly recognise himself. After studying the effect in the mirror from all possible angles, Paddington

decided to try it out downstairs. It was difficult to walk properly; Jonathan's old coat was too long for him and he kept treading on it. Apart from that, his ears didn't seem to fit the beard as well as he would have liked, so that he had to hang on to it with one paw while he went backwards down the stairs, holding on to the banisters with the other paw. He was so intent on what he was doing that he didn't hear Mrs Bird coming up until she was right on top of him.

Mrs Bird looked most startled when she bumped into him. "Oh, Paddington," she began, "I was just coming to see you. I wonder if you would mind going down to the market for me and fetching half a pound of butter?"

"I'm not Paddington," said a gruff voice from behind the beard. "I'm Sherlock Holmes – the famous detective!"

"Yes, dear," said Mrs Bird. "But don't forget the butter. We need it for lunch." With that she turned and went back down the stairs towards the kitchen. The door shut behind her and Paddington heard the murmur of voices.

He pulled off the beard disappointedly. "Thirty-five buns' worth!" he said bitterly, to no one in particular. He almost felt like going back to the shop and asking for his money back. Thirty-five buns were thirty-five buns and it had taken him a long time to save that much money.

But when he got outside the front door Paddington hesitated. It seemed such a pity to waste his disguise, and even if Mrs Bird had seen through it, Mr Briggs, the foreman at the building site, might not. Paddington decided to have one more try. He might even pick up some more clues.

By the time he arrived at the new house he was feeling much more pleased with himself. Out of the corner of his eye he had noticed quite a number of people staring at him as he passed. And when he'd looked at them over the top of his glasses several of them had hurriedly crossed to the other side of the road.

He crept along outside the house until he heard voices. They seemed to be coming from an open window on the first floor and he distinctly recognised Mr Briggs's voice among them. There was a ladder propped against the wall and Paddington clambered up the rungs until his head was level with the window-sill. Then he carefully peered over the edge.

Mr Briggs and his men were busy round a small stove making themselves a cup of tea. Paddington stared hard at Mr Briggs, who was in the act of pouring some water into the teapot, and then, after adjusting his beard, he blew a long blast on his police whistle.

There was a crash of breaking china as Mr Briggs jumped up. He pointed a trembling hand in the direction of the window.

"Cor!" he shouted. "Look! H'an apparition!" The others followed his gaze with open mouths. Paddington stayed just long enough to see four white faces staring at him and then he slid down the ladder on all four paws and hid behind a pile of bricks. Almost immediately there was the sound of excited voices at the window.

"Can't see it now," said a voice. "Must 'ave vanished."

"Cor!" repeated Mr Briggs, mopping his brow with a spotted handkerchief. "Whatever it was, I don't never want to see nothing like it again. Fair chilled me to the marrow it did!" With that he slammed the window shut and the voices died away.

From behind the pile of bricks Paddington could hardly believe his ears. He had never even dreamed that Mr Briggs and his men could be mixed up in the affair. And yet – he had definitely heard Mr Briggs say his marrow had been chilled.

After removing his beard and dark glasses, Paddington sat down behind the bricks and made several notes in his book with the invisible ink. Then he made his way slowly and thoughtfully in the direction of the grocer's.

It had been a very good day's detecting, and Paddington decided he would have to pay another visit to the building site when all was quiet.

It was midnight. All the household had long since gone to bed.

"You know," said Mrs Brown, just as the

clock was striking twelve, "it's a funny thing, but I'm sure Paddington's up to something."

"There's nothing funny in that," replied Mr Brown sleepily. "He's always up to *something*. What is it this time?"

"That's just the trouble," said Mrs Brown. "I don't really know. But he was wandering around wearing a false beard this morning. He nearly startled poor Mrs Bird out of her wits. He's been writing things in his notebook all the evening too, and do you know what?"

"No," said Mr Brown, stifling a yawn. "What?"

"When I looked over his shoulder there was nothing there!"

"Oh well, bears will be bears," said Mr Brown. He paused for a moment as he reached up to turn out the light. "That's strange," he said. "I could have sworn I heard a police whistle just then."

"Nonsense, Henry," said Mrs Brown. "You must be dreaming."

Mr Brown shrugged his shoulders as he turned out the light. He was much too tired to argue. All the same he knew he *had* heard a whistle. But as he closed his eyes and prepared himself for sleep, it never crossed his mind that the cause of it might be Paddington.

Lots of things had been happening to Paddington since he'd crept out of the Browns'

house under cover of darkness and made his way round to the building site. So many things had happened, one after the other, that he almost wished he'd never decided to be a detective in the first place. He felt very glad when, in answer to several loud blasts on his whistle, a large black car drew up at the side of the road and two men in uniform got out.

"Hallo, hallo," said the first of the men, looking hard at Paddington. "What's going on here?"

Paddington pointed a paw dramatically in the direction of the new house. "I've captured a burglar!" he announced.

"A *what?*" asked the second policeman, peering at Paddington. He'd come across some very strange things in the course of duty, but he'd never been called out in the middle of the night by a young bear before. This one seemed to be wearing a long black beard and a duffle coat. It was most unusual.

"A burglar," repeated Paddington. "I think he's the one that took Mr Brown's marrow!"

"Mr Brown's marrow?" repeated the first policeman, looking rather dazed as he followed Paddington through his secret entrance into the house.

"That's right," said Paddington. "Now he's got my marmalade sandwiches. I took a big parcel of them inside with me in case I got hungry while I was waiting."

"Of course," said the second policeman, trying to humour Paddington. "Marmalade sandwiches." He tapped his forehead as he looked at his colleague. "And where is the burglar now – eating your sandwiches?"

"I expect so," said Paddington. "I shut him in the room and I put a piece of wood under the door so that he couldn't get out. I got my beard caught in one of the sandwiches – so I switched my torch on to take some of the hairs out of the marmalade and then it happened!"

"What happened?" chorused the policemen. They were finding it rather difficult to keep up with Paddington's description of the course of events.

"I saw someone flashing a light outside the window," explained Paddington, as patiently as he could. "Then I heard footsteps coming up the stairs, so I lay in wait." He pointed towards a door at the top of the stairs. "He's in there!"

Before either of the policemen could ask any more questions there came the sound of banging and a voice cried, "Let me out!"

"Good heavens!" exclaimed the first policeman. "There *is* someone in there." He looked at Paddington with renewed respect. "Did you get a description, sir?"

"He was about eight feet tall," said Paddington, recklessly, "and he sounded very cross when he found he couldn't get out."

"Hmm!" said the second policeman. "Well, we'll soon see about that. Stand back!" With that he pulled the piece of wood from under the door and flung it open, shining his torch into the room.

Everyone stood back and waited for the worst to happen. To their surprise, when the man came out it was another policeman.

"Locked in!" he exclaimed bitterly. "I see some lights flashing from an empty house, so I go to investigate… and what happens? I'm locked in… by a *bear*!" He pointed towards Paddington. "And if I'm not mistaken, that's him!"

Paddington suddenly began to feel very small. All three policemen were looking at him, and in the excitement his beard had fallen off one ear.

"Hmm," said the first policeman. "And what were *you* doing in an empty house at gone midnight, young fellow-me-bear? And wearing a disguise at that! I can see we shall have to take you along to the station for questioning."

"It's a bit difficult to explain," said Paddington, sadly. "I'm afraid it's going to take rather a long time. You see... it's all to do with Mr Brown's marrow – the one he was going to enter for the vegetable show..."

The policemen weren't the only ones who found it all rather hard to understand. Mr Brown was still asking questions long after Paddington had been returned from the police station to the family's safe keeping.

"I still don't see how my losing a marrow has got anything to do with Paddington being arrested," he said for the hundredth time.

"But Paddington wasn't arrested, Henry," said Mrs Brown. "He was only detained for questioning. Anyway, he was only trying to get your marrow back for you. You ought to be very grateful."

She sighed. She would have to tell her husband the truth sooner or later. She'd already told Paddington. "I'm afraid it's all my fault really," she said. "You see... *I* cut your marrow by mistake!"

"*You* did?" exclaimed Mr Brown. "You cut my prize marrow?"

"Well, I didn't realise it was your prize one," said Mrs Brown. "And you know how fond you are of stuffed marrow. We had it for dinner last night!"

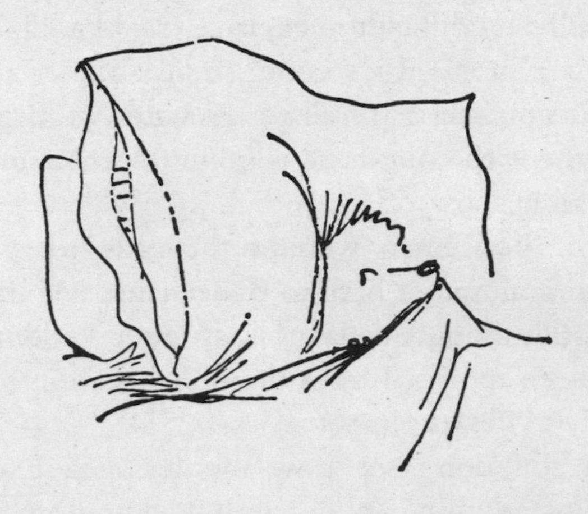

Back in his own room, Paddington felt quite pleased with himself as he got into bed. He'd have a lot to tell his friend, Mr Gruber in the morning. Once the inspector at the police station had heard his full story he had complimented Paddington on his bravery and ordered his immediate release.

"I wish there were more bears about like you, Mr Brown," he had said. And he had given Paddington a real police whistle as a souvenir. Even the policeman who had been locked in said he quite understood how it had all come about.

Besides, he had solved the mystery of the flashing lights at last. It hadn't been anyone in the garden at all, but simply the reflection of his own torch on the window. When he stood up on the end of the bed he could even see himself quite plainly in the glass.

In a way Paddington was sorry about the marrow. Especially as he wouldn't get the reward. But he was very glad the culprit hadn't been Mr Briggs. He liked Mr Briggs – and besides, he'd been promised a ride in his bucket. He didn't want to miss that.

A Spot of Fishing

from *Paddington Abroad*

A Spot of Fishing

"How about a spot of fishing today?" asked Mr Brown at breakfast one morning.

Mr Brown's query was greeted in various ways by the other members of the family. Mrs Brown and Mrs Bird exchanged anxious glances, Jonathan and Judy let out whoops of delight, while Paddington nearly fell off his seat with excitement.

"What are we going to fish for?" asked Mrs Brown, hoping her husband might suggest something safe near the seashore.

"Mackerel," said Mr Brown vaguely. "Or we might even try for some sardines. Anyway, all those in favour raise their right hand."

Mr Brown looked pleased at the response to

his idea. "That's four to two in favour," he said.

"It's two all," said Mrs Bird sternly. "Bears who raise both their paws at the same time are disqualified."

"Well, I haven't voted yet," said Mr Brown, putting up his own hand, "so that's still three to two.

"There's a nice little island just outside the bay," he continued. "We can sail out there and make it our base."

"Did you say *sail* out there, Henry?" asked Mrs Brown nervously.

"That's right," said Mr Brown. "I met Admiral Grundy just before breakfast and he's invited us out for the day."

Mrs Brown and Mrs Bird began to look even less enthusiastic at Mr Brown's last remark, and even Paddington's whiskers drooped noticeably into his roll and marmalade.

Admiral Grundy was a retired English naval officer who lived in a house called the Crow's Nest on the cliffs just outside the village. The Browns had met him on one or two occasions and he had a voice like a rusty fog-horn which always made them rather nervous.

The first time he had bellowed at them so loudly from the top of the cliff that Mrs Brown had been quite worried in case there was a fall of rock, and Paddington had dropped an ice-cream cone into the sea in his fright.

"Been watchin' you for the last three days through me telescope," he'd roared at Mr Brown. "Knew by your shorts you must be English. Though I saw a bear gallivantin' about on the beach. Couldn't believe me eyes!"

"I think his bark's worse than his bite," said Mr Brown. "And he seems very keen on our going out with him. I don't suppose he sees many English people now he's retired."

"H'mm!" said Mrs Bird mysteriously. "I can see we've got some preparations to make." And with that she left the table and disappeared upstairs only to return a few minutes later armed with a small parcel which she handed to Paddington.

"Something told me we might be going

sailing," she said. "Sea-water makes bears' fur sticky, so I made a sea-going outfit before we left out of one of Jonathan's old cycling capes."

Paddington gasped with astonishment when he untied the parcel and saw what was inside, and everyone stood round admiring while he donned a pair of oilskin leggings, a jacket and a sou'wester.

"Thank you very much, Mrs Bird," he said gratefully, as he made some final adjustments to his braces.

"That settles it," said Mr Brown. "We shall simply *have* to go sailing now!"

After they had collected their belongings the Browns made their way down the winding cobbled street leading to the harbour and Paddington followed them in a daze. To have one surprise was a nice way to start any day, but to be told he was going sailing *and* to have a new outfit at the same time was doubly exciting.

Paddington was very keen on boats and harbours, and he liked the one at St Castille in particular for it was quite different to anything he had ever seen before in his travels. For one thing the fishermen used most unusual light blue nets which looked very jolly when they were hung out to dry. And even the men themselves were different, for instead of wearing dark blue jerseys and rubber boots like most fishermen, they had red jackets and wooden clogs called 'sabots'.

Paddington had spent a lot of his time sitting on the quayside with the Browns watching the activities in the harbour as the sardine boats came and went, and he was looking forward to the day's outing.

Admiral Grundy was already on board his yacht when the Browns arrived, and as they rounded the corner he gave a start and then fixed Paddington with a steely look from beneath his bushy eyebrows.

"Shiver me timbers!" he exploded. "What's this? Expectin' a gale?"

"Shiver your timbers, Mr Grundy?" exclaimed Paddington with interest. He peered hard at the Admiral's boat but it appeared to be all in one piece and the planks seemed well stuck together.

"I think he's surprised at your oilskins," whispered Judy, as the Admiral looked up at the sun and then back at Paddington.

"My oilskins?" said Paddington hotly, giving the Admiral a hard stare back. "They're some of Mrs Bird's specials!"

Recovering himself, the Admiral held out his hand gallantly to Mrs Bird. "Welcome aboard, ma'am," he exclaimed. "Hope I haven't offended you. Come along now. Women and bears first."

"You can go up for'ard, bear," he said as Paddington clambered aboard. "Keep a sharp look-out – and listen for me instructions."

After touching the brim of his sou'wester with his paw, Paddington hurried along the deck until he reached the front of the boat. He wasn't quite sure what he was supposed to look out for but he felt very pleased he'd brought his opera-glasses along and he spent several moments peering through them at the horizon.

Although he didn't want to offend Mrs Bird after all the trouble she had taken, he was beginning to wish he'd taken Admiral Grundy's advice and kept his sailing outfit until a storm blew up. Apart from the fact that it was a hot day, his braces kept slipping off his shoulders and he had to hold his trousers up with one paw, which made keeping a lookout very difficult.

He was suddenly startled out of his daydreams by a roar from the back of the yacht.

"Stand by for'ard!" bellowed the admiral as he inspected his ship.

"Watch the burgee," he shouted, pointing to a small triangular flag which flew at the mast-head. "Tells you which way the wind's blowin'," he explained to Mrs Bird, who was sheltering in the stern beneath her sunshade. "Most important!

"Get ready to splice the mainbrace down below," he called to Mr Brown, who was somewhere in the cabin. "Stand by to cast off up for'ard, bear!"

From his position in the front of the Admiral's yacht, Paddington was getting more and more confused by all the shouting. Setting sail was much more complicated than he had imagined.

First of all he thought the Admiral had said something about watching a birdy, but the only birds he could see were sea-gulls and most of those seemed to be asleep.

Then the Admiral had bellowed something about splicing his braces.

Paddington was most surprised by the last order for although his trousers were getting lower and lower, he hadn't realised anyone else had noticed and he hastily picked up a coil of rope and began tying it round his middle to be on the safe side.

"Stand by!" bellowed the Admiral. "I'm goin' to haul up me mainsail.

"Nothin' like a good sailin' craft," he continued with satisfaction as he pulled away at the rope. "Can't stand engines meself."

"I must say it's a lovely sight," began Mrs Brown as the large white sail billowed out in the breeze. She broke off and stared at the Admiral. "Is anything the matter?" she asked.

"Where's that young bear feller of yours got to?" exploded the Admiral. "Don't tell me he's fallen overboard!"

"Good gracious!" exclaimed Mrs Bird anxiously. "Where on earth can he have got to?"

The Browns looked over the side into the

water but there was neither sight nor sound of Paddington.

"Can't see any bubbles," said the Admiral. "And as for hearin' anything – couldn't hear a ship's siren with all that jabberin' goin' on ashore – let alone a bear's cries!"

The Browns looked up. Now that the Admiral mentioned it, there did seem to be a lot of noise going on. Quite a number of the fishermen on the quay were waving their arms and several were pointing up at the sky.

"Good grief!" exploded the Admiral as he stood up and shaded his eyes against the sun. "He's up aloft. Got himself hoisted to me mainmast!"

"I was only splicing my braces," gasped Paddington, looking most offended as he was lowered back down on to the deck. "I was having trouble with my oilskins and I think I must have picked up the wrong rope by mistake."

"I think," said Mrs Bird, quickly pouring oil on troubled waters before the Admiral had time to speak, "you'd better sit in the back with me out of harm's way."

Already quite a large crowd had collected on the quayside and she didn't like the look on the Admiral's face. It seemed to have gone a rather nasty shade of purple.

Paddington dusted himself down and then

settled thankfully in the seat alongside Mrs Bird while order was restored and the Admiral once more made ready to sail.

Within a matter of moments everything was ship-shape and before long they found themselves skimming through the open water outside the harbour.

While Jonathan and Judy sat on the deck watching the wash of the wave breaking over the bow of the yacht, Mr Brown set up his rod and line, and even Paddington had a go over the stern with a piece of string and a bent pin which Mrs Bird found in her handbag.

It was all so new and interesting that it seemed no time at all before they found themselves on the island.

Apart from all the Admiral's things, Mr Brown

had brought along a tent and a large hamper of food which Mrs Bird had bought in the village store, and while Jonathan, Judy and Paddington made ready to explore the island, the Admiral and Mr Brown began unloading the yacht.

It was as they turned to go back for their second trip that the Admiral suddenly let out an extra loud bellow and began pointing out to sea as he danced up and down the beach.

"It's adrift!" he cried. "Me yacht's adrift!"

The Browns followed the direction of the Admiral's gaze with alarm only to see the yacht dancing on the waves some distance away as it headed out to sea.

"Shiver me timbers!" roared the Admiral. "Didn't anyone tie it up?"

The Browns looked at each other. In the excitement of landing on the island they had left it to the Admiral.

"We thought you'd done it," said Mr Brown.

"Fifty years at sea," growled the Admiral, stomping up and down the beach. "Never lost a ship yet, let alone been marooned. What a crew!"

"Can't you send up a distress signal or something?" asked Mrs Brown unhappily.

"Can't," growled the Admiral. "Me flares are on board!"

"So are my matches," said Mr Brown. "So we

can't even light a bonfire."

Admiral Grundy stomped up and down the beach several more times growling to himself before he stopped and pointed to Mr Brown's tent. "I'll set up me headquarters on the grass at the top of the beach," he exclaimed. "Must have a bit of peace and quiet while I think up some way of letting the johnnies on the mainland know what's happened."

"I'll help if you like, Mr Grundy," said Paddington, anxious to lend a paw.

"Thank you, bear," said the Admiral gruffly. "But you'll have to be careful with your knots. Don't want it blowin' over as soon as I get inside."

Leaving the Browns in a forlorn group on the beach as they discussed the prospect of spending a night on the island, the Admiral picked up the tent and headed towards the top of the beach closely followed by Paddington.

Paddington was very interested in the subject of Mr Brown's tent. He had come across it once or twice when he'd been exploring the attic at Windsor Gardens, but he'd never seen it in use before. When they reached the grass he sat down on a nearby rock and watched carefully while the Admiral undid the carrying case and spread a large sheet of white canvas over the ground,

together with several lengths of wooden pole and a number of ropes.

After joining the wooden poles together into two lengths, the Admiral fitted the canvas sheet over them and then lifted the whole lot into the air.

"I'll hold the poles, bear," he roared as he disappeared inside, "if you'll fix the guy-ropes. You'll find some stakes in the bag."

Paddington jumped up from the rock. He wasn't at all sure what guy-ropes were, let alone stakes, but he was glad to be able to do something useful at last, and as he hurried forward and peered in the bag he was even more pleased to see that as well as a mallet and some pieces of wood there was a book of instructions.

Paddington liked instruction books – especially when there were plenty of pictures – and Mr Brown's seemed to have a great many. On the cover there was one which showed a man hammering the pieces of wood into the ground, and although the man in the picture wore shorts and was fat and jolly – not a bit like the Admiral, who was very gruff – he felt sure it would be a great help.

"What's goin' on, bear?" called the Admiral in a muffled voice. "Shake a leg there. I can't hold on much longer."

Paddington looked up and saw to his surprise that the Admiral and his tent were no longer where they had started off. There was a strong breeze blowing now that they were away from the beach and the Admiral seemed to be having some difficulty in staying upright as the canvas billowed out like a sail.

"Hold on, Mr Grundy," cried Paddington, waving his mallet in the air. "I'm coming."

After consulting the instructions several more times he picked up a pawful of stakes and hurried across to where the Admiral was struggling.

Paddington was keen on hammering and he spent an enjoyable few minutes banging all the stakes into the ground and making fast the various ropes before pulling them tight as the Admiral had told him.

There were a great many ropes, in fact there seemed to be far more than there were in the picture, and Paddington had to make several trips back to the bag for more stakes so that it all took much longer than he had expected.

Apart from that the Admiral kept shouting for him to make haste so that he became more and more confused, and the knots – far from being neat and tidy like the ones in the instructions – began to look more and more like a piece of very old knitting that had gone wrong.

"Is that a new tent?" asked Mrs Bird, as she viewed the goings-on from the beach.

"No," replied Mr Brown. "It's the same old one. Why do you ask?"

"It looks different to me," said Mrs Bird. "It's a very odd shape. Sort of tall and baggy."

"Good heavens!" exclaimed Mr Brown. "You're right."

"I think," said Mrs Bird, "we'd better go and see what's happening. I don't like the look of things at all."

In saying she didn't like the look of things, Mrs

Bird was echoing Paddington's thoughts as well as her own for, having at long last finished banging in all the stakes and tying all the knots, he stood up to admire his handiwork only to find to his surprise that the Admiral was nowhere in sight.

Even the tent looked quite different to the one shown on the last page of the instructions. The one there was not unlike a small house, with the man in shorts looking as fresh as a daisy and smiling all over his face as he stepped out through a door in the side and waved to a crowd of admiring onlookers. As he mopped his brow and looked at Mr Brown's tent, even Paddington had to admit to himself that it was more like a bundle of old washing with several lumps sticking out of the side.

He hurried all the way round peering at it closely, but there was nowhere anyone could possibly crawl through let alone any sign of a door. Worse still, far from there being any sign of a smiling Admiral, he seemed to have disappeared altogether.

Paddington anxiously tapped one of the lumps in the side with his hammer. "Are you there, Mr Grundy?" he called.

"Grr," came an explosion from within. "THAT WAS MY HEAD!"

Paddington jumped back as if he had been shot and nearly fell over one of the guy-ropes in his haste to escape.

"*Let me out, bear*!" roared the Admiral. "*I'll have you in irons for this*!"

Paddington didn't like the sound of being put in irons at all and he hurriedly consulted the instruction book again in case he had turned over two pages at once by mistake, but there wasn't even a section on how to take the tent down again once it was up, let alone anything about missing campers.

He tried pulling hard on the guy-ropes, but it only seemed to make matters worse, and the harder he pulled the more the Admiral bellowed.

"Paddington!" exclaimed Mrs Brown, as they reached him just in time to be greeted by a particularly loud yell from the Admiral. "What on earth's going on?"

"I don't know, Mrs Brown," said Paddington. "I think I must have got my guys crossed. It's a bit difficult with paws."

"Crikey!" said Jonathan admiringly, as he bent down to examine the tent. "I'll say you have. I've never seen knots like these before. Not even in the Scouts."

"Good gracious!" said Mrs Bird. "We'd better do something quickly. He'll suffocate."

One by one the Browns bent down and looked at the ropes, but the more they pulled and tugged the tighter became the knots and the fainter became the Admiral's gurgles.

It was just as they were giving up all hope of ever setting him free that a most unexpected interruption took place. The Browns had been so intent on the problem of untying Paddington's knots that they had quite failed to notice a lot of activity going on on the beach. The first they knew of it was when they heard voices close at hand and they looked up to find a group of fishermen from the village making their way towards them.

"We saw your signal for help, monsieur," said the leader in broken English.

"Our signal for help?" repeated Mr Brown.

"That is right, monsieur," said the fisherman. "We saw it from many miles away. The young English bear from the hotel waving his white sheet in distress. And then we found Monsieur le Admiral's boat adrift so we came to the rescue."

Mr Brown stood back while the fishermen gathered round the tent to inspect the knots. "I wonder whether it's just Paddington," he said. "Or whether all bears are born under a lucky star!"

"Grrmph!" growled the Admiral for the umpteenth time as the story of his rescue was repeated to him.

It had taken even the fishermen some while to undo Paddington's knots, and by the time he was set free the Admiral's face had been the colour of a freshly boiled lobster. But when he heard the news that his yacht had been found and was safely at anchor in the bay he soon grew calm again. As the day wore on he became quite jolly and even joined in a number of games on the beach.

"I suppose I ought to thank you, bear," he growled on the way back, as he held out his hand. "Could have done with a few more of your sort on board me ship in the old days. Enjoyed meself no end."

"That's all right, Mr Grundy," said Paddington, offering his paw in return. He still wasn't quite sure why everyone was thanking him – especially as he had expected to be in trouble – but he wasn't the sort of bear to query his good fortune.

"Suppose you like cocoa?" growled the Admiral suddenly.

Paddington's eyes grew large. "Yes, please," he exclaimed. And even the Browns looked most surprised that the Admiral should know such a thing.

"Haven't travelled the seven seas without learnin' somethin' about bears' habits," said the Admiral.

He shaded his eyes as they entered the harbour

mouth and the setting sun flickered for a moment behind the houses. "Don't suppose you've ever tasted real ship's cocoa," he said. "Make it meself in a bucket. How about comin' up to me cabin for a cup before you go to bed?"

To that the Browns gave an enthusiastic "Aye! Aye!" and even Paddington was allowed to raise both his paws in agreement. It had been a most exciting and enjoyable day, and although they had none of them so much as seen a glimpse of a sardine, let alone caught one, they all agreed there was nothing like a cup of real ship's cocoa to round things off in a proper seamanlike fashion.

An Unexpected Party

from *Paddington Marches On*

An Unexpected Party

Paddington paused on the stairs of number thirty-two Windsor Gardens and sniffed the morning air. A few moments later, having consulted the Browns' calendar through the banisters, he hurried on his way with a puzzled expression on his face.

There was definitely something mysterious going on that morning and he couldn't for the life of him make out what it was. Unless Mrs Bird had made a mistake when she'd changed the date, which would have been most unusual; and unless he'd also overslept by two or three days, which seemed even more unlikely, it should have been a Thursday – and yet all the signs were Sunday ones.

To start with there was a strong smell of freshly baked cakes coming from the direction of the kitchen and although Mrs Bird occasionally did her baking during the week she was much more inclined to do it on a Sunday. In any case she never made cakes quite so early in the morning.

Then there was the strange behaviour of Mr Brown. Mr Brown worked in the City of London and in the mornings he followed a strict timetable. Breakfast was served punctually at half past eight and before that, come rain or shine, he always took a quick stroll round the garden in order to inspect the flower beds.

On this particular morning Paddington had nearly fallen over backwards with surprise when he'd drawn back his curtains and peered out of the window only to see a very unkempt-looking Mr Brown pushing a wheelbarrow down the garden path.

"I was wondering when you were going to put in an appearance," said Mrs Bird, as Paddington poked his head round the kitchen door with an inquiring look on his face. "I've never known such a bear for smelling out things."

Mrs Bird hastily closed the oven door before Paddington could see inside and then began dishing up his breakfast. "Don't go eating too much," she warned. "We're having a party this afternoon and I've enough to feed a regiment of bears."

"A party!" exclaimed Paddington, looking more and more surprised. Paddington liked parties. Since he'd been with the Browns they'd had quite a number of Christmas and birthday ones, but it was most unusual to have a party in between times.

"Never you mind," said Mrs Bird mysteriously, when he inquired what it was all about. "It's a party – that's all you need to know. And don't go getting egg all over your whiskers," she warned. "Mr Gruber's been invited, *and* Mr Curry – not to mention quite a few other people."

Paddington carried his plate of bacon and eggs into the dining-room and settled himself at the table with a thoughtful expression on his face. The more he considered the matter the more mysterious it seemed. The most surprising thing of all was that the Browns' next-door neighbour had received an invitation, and Paddington decided it must be a very important occasion indeed. Mr Curry often turned up at the Browns' parties but almost always it was because he'd asked himself and very rarely because he'd actually been invited.

Jonathan and Judy were most unhelpful as well. They came into the dining-room to say good morning while Paddington was having his breakfast but as soon as he asked what was going on they both hurried out of the room again.

"It's a special party, Paddington," said Judy, squeezing his paw as she left. "Just for you. But don't worry – you'll find out all about it later on."

Even Mr Gruber quickly changed the subject when Paddington asked him all about it later that morning.

"I think it's meant to be a bit of a surprise, Mr Brown," was all he would say. "And a surprise wouldn't be a surprise if you knew what it was."

Before any more questions could be asked Mr Gruber hastily broke a bun in two and gave one half to Paddington before disappearing into the darkness at the back of his shop in order to make the morning cocoa.

When he returned he was carrying a large book on the cocoa tray. "I expect we shall be having fun and games this afternoon, Mr Brown," he said, as he handed the book to Paddington. "I thought you might like to have a browse through this. It's a bumper book of party tricks."

Paddington thanked Mr Gruber, and after he had finished his cocoa he hurried back in the direction of Windsor Gardens. Mrs Bird had warned him that with a party in the offing there would be a lot of work to do and he didn't want to be late home. Apart from that Mr Gruber's fun book looked very interesting and he was anxious to test some of the tricks before lunch.

But as it happened all thoughts of party games passed completely out of his mind as he reached home.

While he had been out everyone else had been busy and a great change had come over the dining-room. An extra leaf had been put in the table and the snow-white cloth was barely visible beneath all the food. Paddington's eyes grew larger and larger as he took in the dishes of jelly, fruit and cream, and the plates laden with sandwiches and cakes, not to mention mounds

of biscuits and piles of jam and marmalade. In the middle of it all, in a place of honour, was a large iced cake. The cake had some foreign words written across the top but before he had time to make out what they were Mrs Bird discovered him and drove him up to the bathroom.

"You'll have to be at the front door to welcome your guests," she warned. "You can collect as many marmalade stains as you like this afternoon but not before."

With that Paddington had to be content. But as the time for the party drew near he became more and more excited. The Browns had invited not only Mr Gruber and Mr Curry but a number of the traders from the Portobello Road as well. Despite his habit of driving a hard bargain Paddington was a popular bear in the market and by the time all the guests had arrived the Browns' dining-room was full almost to overflowing.

When the last of the visitors had settled themselves comfortably Mr Brown called for silence.

"As you all know," he began, "this is Paddington's party. I have an important announcement to make later on, but first of all I think Paddington himself wants to entertain you with a few special tricks he has up his paw."

Everyone applauded while Paddington took his place on the rug in front of the fireplace and consulted Mr Gruber's book of party games. There was one chapter in particular which he'd had his eye on. It was called ONE HUNDRED DIFFERENT WAYS OF TEARING PAPER and he was looking forward to trying some of them out.

"I like paper-tearing tricks," said Mr Curry, when Paddington explained what he was going to do. "I hope they're good ones, bear."

"I think the first one is, Mr Curry," replied Paddington. "It's called THE MYSTERY OF THE DISAPPEARING TEN POUND NOTE!"

"Oh dear," said Mrs Brown nervously. "Must it be a ten pound note? Couldn't you use something else?"

Paddington peered at his book again. "It doesn't say you can," he replied doubtfully. "But I expect I could make do with a five pound one."

"I'm afraid I've left my wallet in my other jacket," said Mr Brown hastily.

"And I've only got silver," said Mr Gruber, taking the hint as all Paddington's other friends from the market hurriedly buttoned their jackets.

Everyone turned and looked towards Mr Curry. "You did say you like paper-tearing tricks," said Mr Brown meaningly. "And it *is* Paddington's party."

Mr Curry took a deep breath as he withdrew his purse from an inside pocket and undid the clasp. "I hope you know what you're doing, bear," he growled, handing Paddington a five pound note.

"Crikey! So do I!" whispered Jonathan as Paddington took the note and after consulting his book once more folded it in half and began tearing pieces out.

The Browns watched anxiously while Paddington folded the note yet again and Mr Curry's face got blacker and blacker at the sight of all the pieces fluttering to the floor.

After a slight pause Paddington took another look at his book and as he did so his expression changed. Whereas a moment before he had seemed full of confidence, now his whiskers drooped and a worried look came over his face.

"What are you doing now, bear?" growled Mr Curry as Paddington hurried over and began peering in his ear.

"I'm afraid something's gone wrong with my trick, Mr Curry," said Paddington unhappily.

"What!" bellowed Mr Curry, jumping to his feet. "What do you mean – *something's gone wrong with it*?"

"The note's supposed to turn up in your ear," explained Paddington, looking more and more unhappy.

"Perhaps it's in the other one, dear," said Mrs Brown hopefully.

"I don't think so," replied Paddington. "I think I must have turned over two pages at once in my instructions. I've been doing the paper doily trick by mistake."

"The paper doily trick," repeated Mr Curry bitterly, as Paddington unfolded the remains of his note and held it up for everyone to see. "My five pound note turned into a bear's doily!"

"Never mind," said Mrs Bird, bending down to pick up the pieces. "If you stick them together perhaps they'll change it at the bank."

"It looks very pretty," said Judy.

Mr Curry snorted several times as he helped himself to a cake. "I've had enough of that bear's paper-tearing tricks for one day," he exclaimed.

Mr Gruber gave a slight cough. "Perhaps you could try one of the other chapters, Mr Brown," he said. "I believe there's a very good one at the end of the book."

"Thank you very much, Mr Gruber," said Paddington gratefully. Mr Curry wasn't the only one who was tired of paper-tearing tricks. Tearing paper, especially banknotes when they were folded, was much more difficult than it sounded, and his paws were beginning to ache.

"There's a very good trick here," he announced after a short pause. "It's called REMOVING A GUEST'S WAISTCOAT WITHOUT TAKING OFF HIS COAT."

"It sounds rather a long trick," said Mrs Brown doubtfully. "Isn't there anything shorter?"

"Nonsense!" said Mr Curry, from behind a plate of sandwiches. "It's a very good trick. I saw it done once years ago in the theatre. I'd like to see it again."

Mr Brown and Mr Gruber exchanged glances. "I'm afraid it'll have to be your waistcoat then," said Mr Brown. "You're the only person who's wearing one."

Mr Curry's jaws dropped. "What!" he exclaimed. "If you think that bear's going to remove my waistcoat you're…"

Whatever else Mr Curry had been about to say was drowned in a roar of protests from the others.

"You said you wanted to see it again," called out the man from the cut-price grocers. "Now's your chance."

With very bad grace Mr Curry got up from his chair and knelt on the rug in front of the fireplace with his arms raised while Paddington put his paws down behind his neck.

"I thought you said you were going to remove my waistcoat, bear," he gurgled, "not choke me with it."

"Well, it's half off anyway," said Mr Brown, as Paddington pulled the waistcoat over Mr Curry's head until it rested under his chin. "What happens now?"

Paddington put his paw up one of Mr Curry's sleeves and began searching. "I'm not quite sure, Mr Brown," he gasped. "I haven't practised this trick before and I can't see the book from where I am."

"Oh dear," said Mrs Brown, as there came a loud tearing noise and Paddington pulled something out of Mr Curry's sleeve. "That looks like a piece of lining."

"What!" bellowed Mr Curry, struggling to see what was going on. "Did you say *lining*?"

Mr Brown picked up the book of party games and adjusted his glasses. "Perhaps I'd better give you a hand, Paddington," he said.

After a moment he put the book down again and knelt on the rug. "You're quite right," he said, feeling up Mr Curry's sleeve. "It definitely says you should pull the end of the waistcoat down the sleeve, but it doesn't say how you do it. It's very odd."

Mr Gruber joined the others on the rug. "Perhaps if we work backwards it might help," he suggested.

"I think you ought to do something quickly," said Mrs Brown anxiously as Mr Curry gave another loud gurgle.

Mr Gruber studied Paddington's book carefully. "Oh dear," he exclaimed. "I hate to tell you this, Mr Brown, but one of the pages appears to be missing."

Mr Curry's eyes bulged and he gave a loud spluttering noise as he took in Mr Gruber's words. "What's that?" he bellowed, jumping to his feet. "I've never heard of such a thing!"

"I don't think you should have done that," said Mr Gruber reprovingly. "It sounded as though you split your coat."

Mr Curry danced up and down with rage as he examined the remains of his jacket. "*I* split it!" he cried. "I like that. And what was that bear doing at the time, I'd like to know?"

"He wasn't anywhere near," said Mrs Bird.

"I was looking for my missing page, Mr Curry," explained Paddington. "I think I must have used it by mistake when I was practising one of my paper-tearing tricks."

Mr Brown held up his hand for silence. Mr Curry's face had changed from red to purple back to an even deeper shade of red again and it looked very much as if it was high time to call a halt to the proceedings. "I'm sure Mrs Bird can mend it for you later on," he said. "But now I think we ought to get down to the business in hand."

"Hear! Hear!" echoed a voice in the audience.

Mr Brown turned to Paddington. "Do you know how long you've been with us now?" he asked.

"I don't know, Mr Brown," said Paddington, looking most surprised at the question. "It feels like always."

"Nearly three years," replied Mr Brown. "Which is quite a long time considering you only came to tea in the first place.

"Now," he continued, when the laughter had died down, "we have a surprise for you. The other day we had a telegram all the way from the Home for Retired Bears in Lima. It seems that Aunt Lucy is celebrating her hundredth birthday very soon and the warden thought it would be a nice idea if all her family could be there with her."

"Fancy being a hundred!" exclaimed Jonathan. "That's jolly old."

"Bears' years are different," said Mrs Bird.

"They have two birthdays a year for a start," said Judy.

"Anyway, Paddington," said Mr Brown, "however many years it is, she's obviously very old and it's a big occasion, so we wondered if you would like to go."

"Speech!" cried someone at the back of the room.

Paddington thought for a moment. "Will I have to travel in a lifeboat and live on marmalade like I did when I came?" he asked.

"No," said Mr Brown, amid more laughter. "I've been to see one of the big shipping companies and they've promised to give you a cabin all to yourself this time at special bear rates and a steward who knows all about these things to look after you."

Paddington sat down on his chair and considered the

matter. Everything had come as such a surprise and his mind was in such a whirl he didn't know quite what to say apart from thanking everyone.

"I shouldn't say anything," said Mrs Bird. "I should have a piece of cake instead. I've made one specially."

"It's got *bon voyage* written on it," explained Judy. "That means we all hope you have a good journey."

"Come on," said the man from the cut price grocers, as Paddington began cutting the cake. "Let's have a chorus of 'For he's a jolly good bear cub'."

For the next few minutes number thirty-two Windsor Gardens echoed and re-echoed to the sound of singing as Paddington handed round pieces of cake and it was noticeable that even Mr Curry sang, "And so say all of us" as loudly as anyone.

"It'll seem quiet without you, bear," he said gruffly, when he paused at the front door some time later and shook Paddington's paw. "I don't know who'll do my odd jobs for me."

"Oh dear," sighed Mrs Brown, as one by one the guests departed until only Mr Gruber was left. "Everything feels so flat now. I do hope we've done the right thing."

"No more marmalade stains on the walls," said Mr Brown, trying to sound a cheerful note, but failing miserably as Paddington hurried upstairs leaving the others to make their way back to the dining-room.

"I shall leave them on," said Mrs Bird decidedly. "I'm not having them washed off for anyone."

"Well, I think you're doing the right thing," said Mr Gruber wisely. "After all, Paddington's Aunt Lucy did bring him up and if it hadn't been for her sending him out into the world we should never have met him."

"I know what you're thinking, Mary," said Mr Brown taking his wife's arm. "But if Paddington does decide to stay in Peru we can't really stand in his way."

The Browns fell silent. When the telegram from Peru first arrived it had seemed a splendid idea to let Paddington go back there for the celebrations, but now that things were finally settled an air of gloom descended over everyone.

In the few years he'd spent with them, Paddington had become so much a part of things it was almost impossible to picture life without him. The thought of their perhaps never seeing him again caused their faces to grow longer and longer.

Their silence was suddenly broken into by a familiar patter of feet on the stairs and a bump as the dining-room door was pushed open and Paddington entered carrying his leather suitcase.

"I've packed my things," he announced. "But I've left my flannel out in case I want a wash before I go."

"Your things?" repeated Mrs Bird. "But what about all the rest of the stuff in your room?"

"You'll need a trunk for that," said Judy.

Paddington looked most surprised. "I'm only taking my important things," he explained. "I thought I'd leave the rest here for safety."

The Browns and Mr Gruber exchanged glances. "Paddington," said Mrs Brown. "Come and sit down. You may not have made much of a speech at the party but you couldn't have chosen anything nicer to say to us now. You'll never know what it means."

"I know one thing it does mean," said Mrs Bird. "I can wash those marmalade stains off the walls now with a clear conscience.

"After all," she added, "we shall need plenty of room for fresh ones when Paddington gets back. That's most important."

In the general agreement which followed Mrs Bird's remark Paddington's voice was the loudest of all.

There was a contented expression on his face as he settled back in his armchair. Although he was most excited at the thought of seeing Aunt Lucy again he was already looking forward to his return, and he felt sure that on a journey all the way to Peru and back he would be able to collect some very unusual stains indeed.

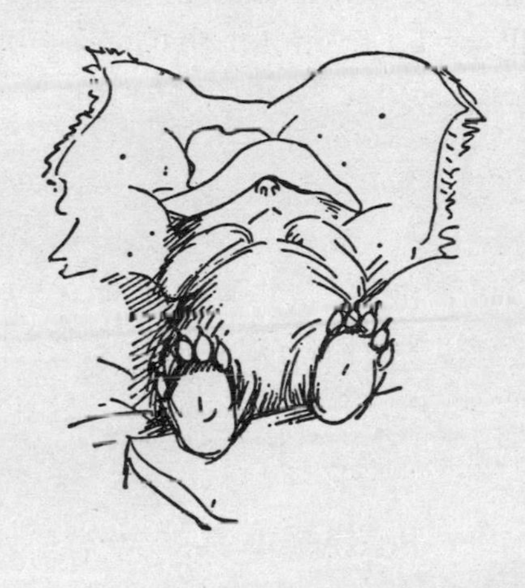

Read Paddington's latest adventure...

Turn the page to enjoy an extract.

Dinner for One

"I do hope we're doing the right thing, Henry," said Mrs Brown as she joined the rest of the family in front of the television set. "I feel all keyed up Paddington's only been gone half an hour and already it feels like an eternity."

"*We're* not doing anything, Mary," said Mr Brown. "For once he's only got himself to blame if anything goes wrong."

"At least they sent a car for him," said Jonathan.

"I can't see what all the fuss is about," said Mr Brown. "It's only a cookery programme after all and they're two a penny these days."

"Dad!" Judy looked at her father pityingly. "It isn't only a cookery programme. It's *Dinner for One.*"

"It's only the best cookery programme ever," agreed Jonathan. "It's broken all records. It topped over ten million viewers last week. Mind you, it wasn't on any of the sports pages so you might have missed it."

"Well, I wouldn't mind a dinner for one myself," said Mr Brown. "Half the office typing pool left off early today. That's why I'm late home."

"Don't worry, Henry," said Mrs Brown. "Yours is in the oven keeping hot. Mrs Bird's just checking to make sure it doesn't get burnt."

"I bet I know why they left off early," said Jonathan, nudging his sister. "The news has reached the City at long last."

"Ever since they raised the winnings they've been sitting up and taking notice," said Judy. "I'm surprised you haven't bought a few shares, Dad."

"Well they must be scraping the barrel a bit if they've invited Paddington to be on the programme," replied Mr Brown defensively. "That's all I can say."

"They didn't invite him," said Mrs Brown. "That's the whole point of it. The contestants apply to be on it and Paddington's application was accepted."

"You mean he *applied*?" said Mr Brown.

"He thought he would surprise us," said Judy. "I think his friend, Mr Gruber, helped him when it came to filling up the form, but it was Paddington's idea. You know how keen he is on anything new and there are some jolly big prizes to be won."

"Well, give him his due," said Mr Brown grudgingly. "Ten out of ten for that. But won't they be in for a bit of a shock? There can't be many bears taking part."

"There's a first time for everything," said Jonathan, "and you get all sorts going in for it. They must be used to it by now."

"The jury stays the same every week," explained Judy. "And there are six different contestants. After a brief chat with the panel to make them feel at home and say who they are and where they come from, they are each given a sealed box of ingredients."

"That part of it is pot luck," broke in Jonathan. "No two boxes are the same."

"Then they are led off to a cooking area," continued Judy, "where all the implements they will need to prepare a main course are ready and waiting, and given fifteen minutes to do it in. It's a real race against time You wait until you see some of the dishes people come up with. It's an absolute hoot."

"In the meantime," said Mr Brown, "I wouldn't mind being led off to our cooking area. Mrs Bird must be getting lonely in the kitchen all by herself."

"Don't worry, Henry," said Mrs Brown. "She'll be out of there like a shot as soon as the programme starts. She won't want to miss a second of it."

The words had hardly left her mouth when a fanfare of trumpeters from the Household Cavalry heralded the start of the programme, and as a banner inscribed DINNER FOR ONE fluttered from a mast and filled the screen Mrs Bird materialised.

"Don't worry," she whispered to Mrs Brown. "Everything's on simmer."

Mr Brown's murmur of "Sounds like the title of a book," fell on deaf ears as the opening preamble to the programme came to an end and the picture on the screen changed to reveal a packed studio audience.

"Good Heavens!" exclaimed Mr Brown, as to a round of frantic applause an aristocratic figure made his way down the centre aisle and up onto the stage to greet the first of the contestants. "There's old Percy Rushmore."

"*Sir* Percival Rushmoor, spelt with two o's," said Mrs Brown.

"There's a lot of money in cast-offs," murmured Mr Brown. "Especially if you make friends with the right people. I wonder what became of his barrow?"

"Shh," hissed Mrs Brown. "Don't spoil it for the others."

"That's Anne Gellica the former TV chef," said Judy, as there was a further round of applause when the camera zoomed in to a head-and-shoulders shot of an elderly lady wearing a chef's white toque hat.

"And that's Ron Keeps, the boxer," said Jonathan, as the camera panned to yet another figure. "It says in a paper I was reading the other day he has a steak for breakfast every day. Two if he has a fight on his hands the same evening."

Mr Brown stifled a groan. "Don't rub it in," he murmured.

"This is my favourite," said Judy, as Ron Keeps shook one fist in the air and then stepped aside to reveal the flamboyant figure of Romney Marsh, the famous gourmet and art historian.

"He always judges a dish by its colour," she said. "Anyone lucky enough to have a bottle of tomato ketchup in their kit is guaranteed another ten points."

"And that last one was Martin Goodbody QC," said Jonathan. "He's a famous lawyer and he's there to make sure there's no hanky-panky going on."

"Hanky-panky?" echoed Mr Brown. "In a cookery programme?"

"You'd be surprised," said Jonathan. "People trying to smuggle their own food in for starters. That kind of thing..."

"Not much gets past him," said Judy. "Someone brought an inflatable marrow in the other week and when he gave it a prod it went off with a bang and everything collapsed. The firemen came rushing on and sprayed the remains…"

She broke off as the cameraman zoomed out and to renewed cheers from the audience a familiar figure dressed in a blue duffle coat and crumpled bush hat brought the arrival of the contestants to an end.

Paddington turned to face the audience and for a brief moment or two appeared to be trying to raise his hat, but to no avail. Seeing his predicament the programme's host came to the rescue.

Hurrying forward, he held out a welcoming hand. "Sir Percival Rushmoor," he said, "I'm invigilating."

"I'm very sorry to hear that, Sir Percival," said Paddington. "I hope you feel better very soon."

Amid laughter from the audience he held out a paw. "Paddington Brown, from Darkest Peru."

"Don't tell me you've come all this way just for a cookery programme," said Sir Percival. "Amazin'. If you find yourself out ridin' in the Cotswolds you must pop in and see me in the family home. You'd be most welcome."

"Thank you very much, Sir Percival," said Paddington. "I live in Windsor Gardens and it's on several bus routes. You would be very welcome there, I'm sure."

"Thanks a heap," said Mr Brown. "How many people did you say watch this programme?"

"Over ten million at the last count," said Jonathan.

"Thank goodness Paddington didn't give him the number of our house," said Mr Brown. "We'd be besieged by photographers if he had."

"Er, thank you very much," said Sir Percival. "I'll make a note of that. Before we begin, tell me, have you had much culinary experience. If so, what is your favourite dish?"

"Mrs Bird lets me have a go sometimes," said Paddington. "And it's chocolate cake."

"How very interesting," said Sir Percival. "Why is that?"

"It doesn't show the dirt," said Paddington.

"Perhaps I won't come to tea after all," said Sir Percival, amid renewed laughter. "And on that happy note I suggest we make a start on our own *Dinner for One*."

To be continued...

A Bear Called
Paddington

Michael Bond

Illustrated by Peggy Fortnum

Paddington Bear had travelled all the way from Darkest Peru when the Brown family first met him on Paddington station. Since then their lives have never been quite the same...

More About
Paddington

Michael Bond

Illustrated by Peggy Fortnum

When Paddington attempts home decorating, detective work and photography, the Brown family soon find that he causes his own particular brand of chaos.

SPONSORED BY

NATIONAL BOOK tokens

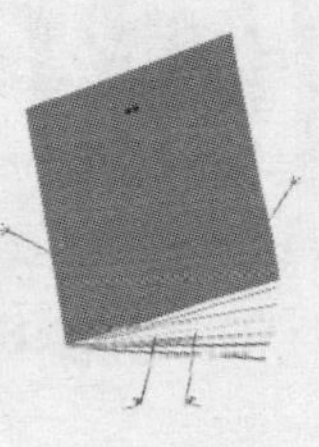

We hope you enjoyed this book.

Proudly brought to you by WORLD BOOK DAY,

the **BIGGEST CELEBRATION** of the **magic** and **fun** of **storytelling**.

We are the **bringer of books to readers** everywhere

and a **charity** on a **MISSION**

to take you on a READING JOURNEY.

EXPLORE new worlds (and bookshops!)

EXPAND your imagination

DISCOVER some of the very best authors and illustrators with us.

A **LOVE OF READING** is one of life's greatest gifts.

And this book is **OUR gift to YOU**.

HAPPY READING.

HAPPY WORLD BOOK DAY!

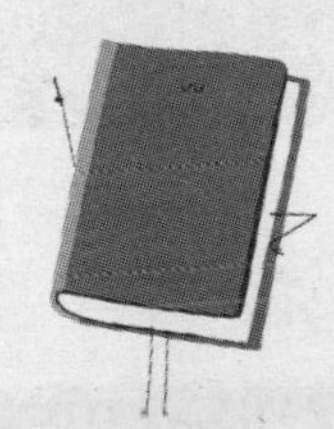

SHARE A STORY

Discover and share stories from breakfast to bedtime.

THREE ways to continue YOUR reading adventure

1 VISIT YOUR LOCAL BOOKSHOP

Your go-to destination for awesome reading recommendations and events with your favourite authors and illustrators.

booksellers.org.uk/bookshopsearch

2 JOIN YOUR LOCAL LIBRARY

Browse and borrow from a huge selection of books, get expert ideas of what to read next and take part in wonderful family reading activities – all for FREE!

findmylibrary.co.uk

3 GO ONLINE AT WORLDBOOKDAY.COM

Fun podcasts, activities, games, videos, downloads, competitions, new books galore and all the latest book news.

Illustrations © Jim Field

SPONSORED B

NATIONAL BOOK tokens

Celebrate stories. Love reading.